Little Gray's Great Migration

by Marta Lindsey

illustrated by Andrea Gabriel

Little Gray popped his head above the
water to look for his favorite thing.

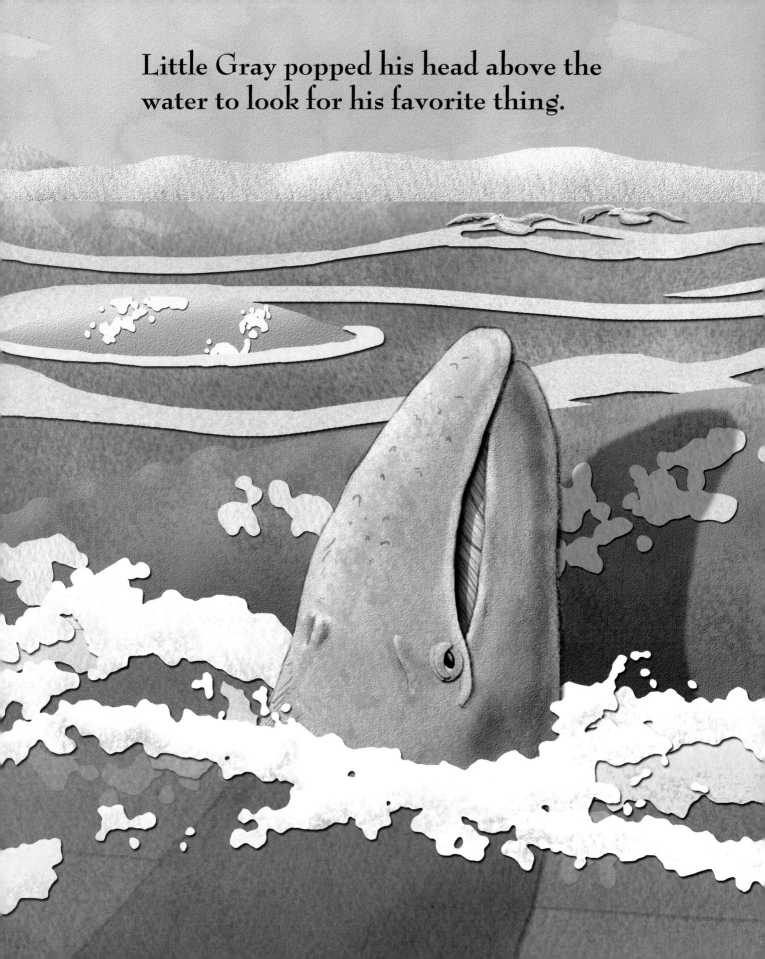

There it was! A boat full of people was on its way into the lagoon.

Little Gray always greeted the people the same way. First, he went right up to the boat for a head rub. *Mmmm!* Next, he blasted bubbles out of his blowhole. *Burbleburble.* Then, he hit the water with his flukes. *Slap, slap, slap!* Finally, Little Gray jumped as high as he could and . . . *SMACK!*

The people clapped and shouted. *Snap, snap, snap!* went their cameras.

One morning, Mama Gray wouldn't let Little Gray greet the people. "It's time for us to swim to the special sea that's filled with food," said Mama.

"Why?" asked Little Gray. "There's plenty for me to eat here." After all, he ate as much of Mama's milk as he wanted.

"The special sea is where you'll learn to eat like a grown-up whale," said Mama. "It's also where we'll make our blubber extra thick before winter, when there's hardly any food."

Little Gray hurried to follow Mama out of the lagoon, but he looked back at the boats the whole time.

The ocean was cold and deep. It was so dark, Little Gray could barely see.

Sometimes they stopped for Little Gray to drink milk. Sometimes they stopped to rest.

But mostly they swam. They swam all day and all night. It was hard work and nothing like the lagoon.

Little Gray missed the people so much! The more he thought about this, the sadder he became . . . and the slower he swam.

Up ahead, land stuck out into the water right in their path. "What should we do?" asked Little Gray. He hoped they would have to go back to the lagoon.

"We'll have to swim around it," said Mama.

Little Gray sighed. But as they swam closer to the land, Little Gray saw something above the waves . . .

. . . People!

Little Gray was so excited he jumped as high as he could. *Smack!* A crowd gathered. *Snap, snap, snap!* went their cameras.

Little Gray jumped again and again. He hadn't known there would be people along the way to the special sea! As they continued on, people watched Little Gray from lighthouses and docks, beaches and boats. The more people he saw, the happier he became . . . and the faster he swam. But then . . .

. . . everything changed. Days went by without seeing any people, and then weeks.

Little Gray got sadder and sadder, and swam slower and slower, until . . . he stopped.

But Mama didn't notice. Soon, Little Gray couldn't see her in the dark waters. "Mama!" squeaked Little Gray. He didn't know which way to go. The water was very quiet. Where was she?

Then Little Gray heard something. *Knock, knock, knock!*

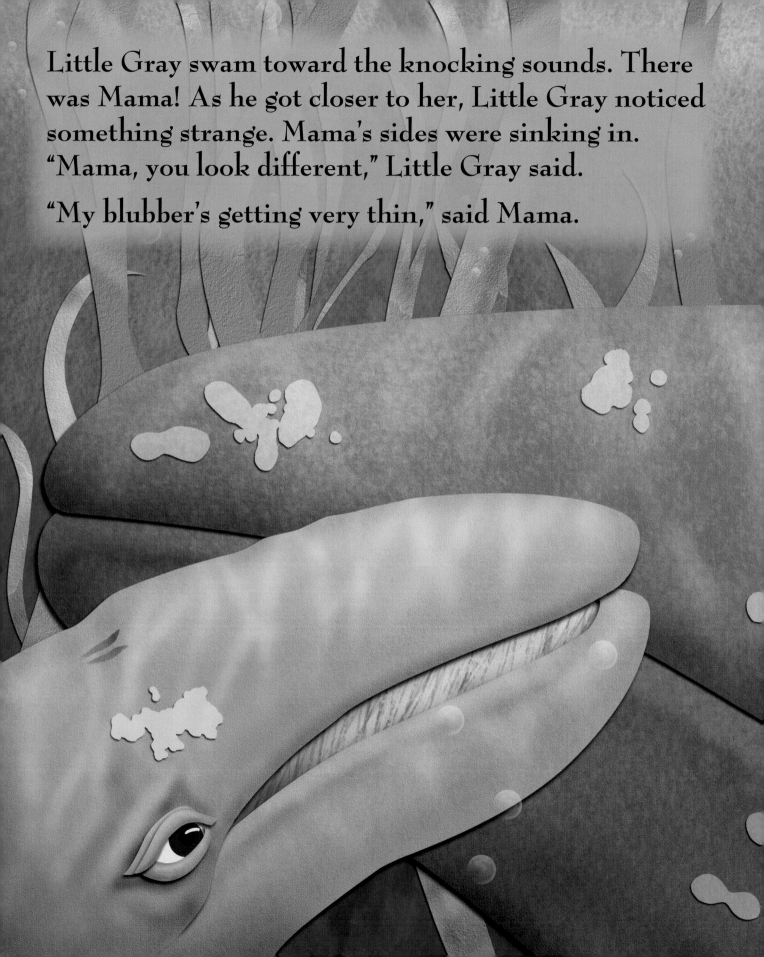

Little Gray swam toward the knocking sounds. There was Mama! As he got closer to her, Little Gray noticed something strange. Mama's sides were sinking in. "Mama, you look different," Little Gray said.

"My blubber's getting very thin," said Mama.

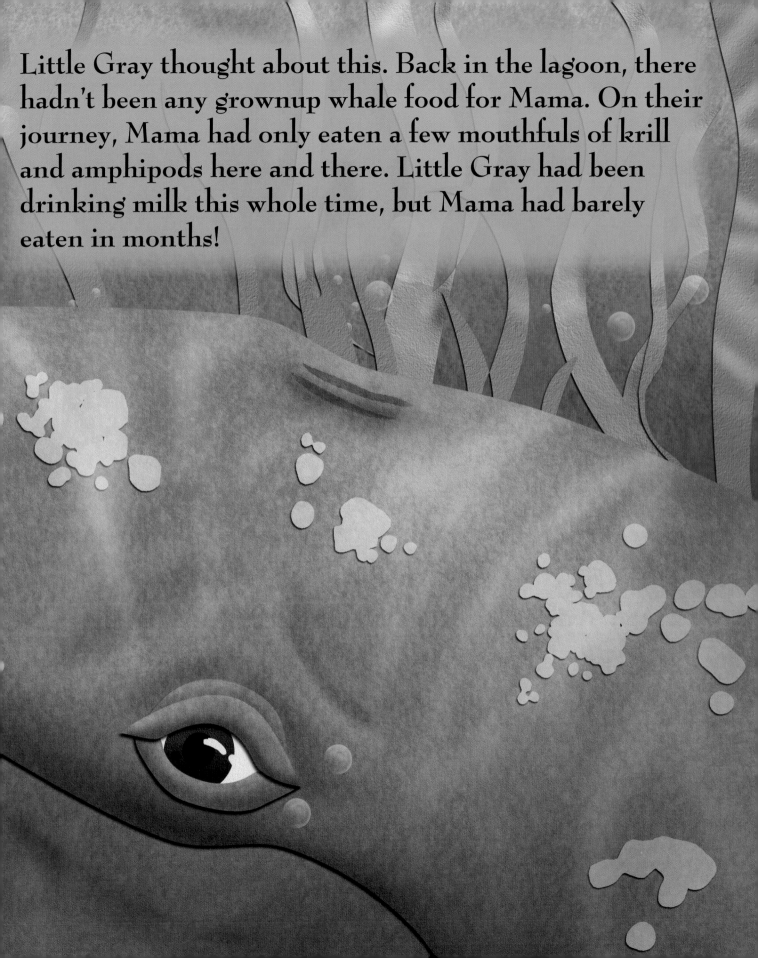

Little Gray thought about this. Back in the lagoon, there hadn't been any grownup whale food for Mama. On their journey, Mama had only eaten a few mouthfuls of krill and amphipods here and there. Little Gray had been drinking milk this whole time, but Mama had barely eaten in months!

From that moment on, Little Gray didn't think about missing the people. He only thought about Mama getting to the special sea. The more he thought about this, the faster he swam. They swam faster and faster, and they were getting closer and closer when . . .

"Oh no!" said Little Gray. Up ahead, a huge piece of land stuck out into the water, blocking their way. Little Gray knew Mama was too weak to make it all the way around the land.

"There's a secret passage," said Mama. "It's a shortcut to the special sea. But I'm so hungry, I'm having trouble remembering where it is."

"I'll find it," said Little Gray.

Little Gray swam back and forth along the land. It all looked the same. What if he couldn't find the passage?

Then Little Gray heard something. It was the knocking and popping sounds of hundreds of other gray whales.

Little Gray followed the sounds
a little farther. There it was. He'd
found the passage!

As they entered the passage, everything changed. The water got greener. The knocking got louder. The passage got wider. Then it opened up to a vast sea.

Right away, Mama dove down to the bottom. Little Gray followed. Mama sucked up a big mouthful of mud. Mama used her tongue to push the mud out through her baleen. *Swoosh!* When Mama opened her mouth, Little Gray could hardly believe what was inside. Mama swallowed it all with one big *gulp!*

Little Gray decided to try. He sucked up a mouthful of mud. *Swoosh! Gulp!* It was pretty different from milk, but . . . *yum!*

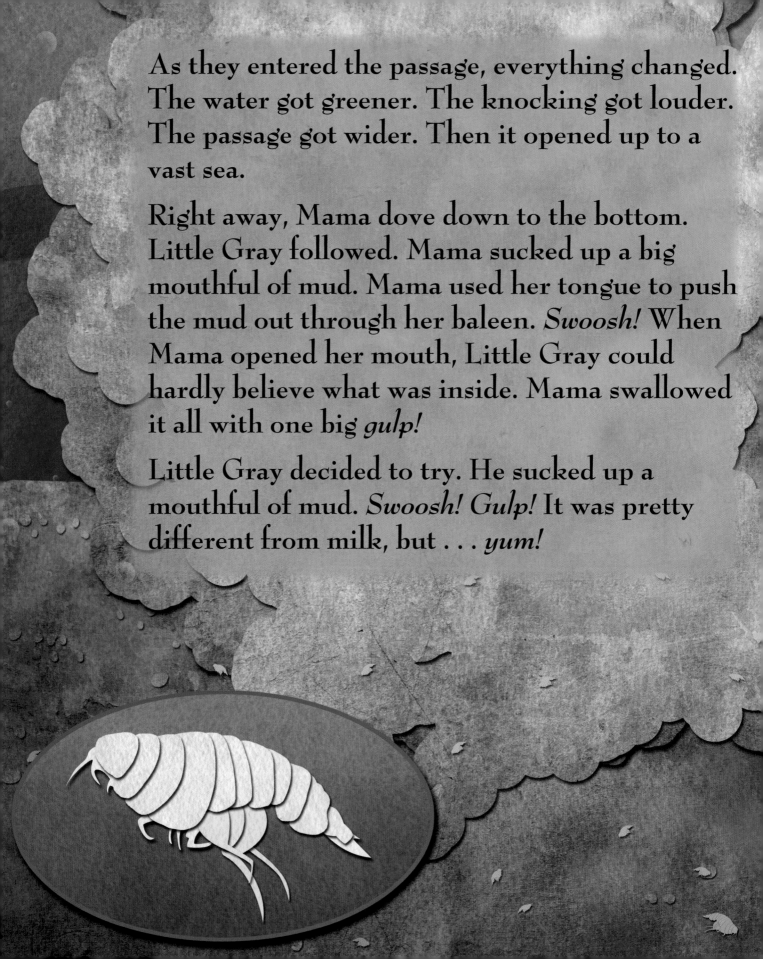

Little Gray popped his head above the water to look around. A sea lion clapped her flippers together. *Whap!* A gull flying above Little Gray squawked. *Caw!* A beluga whale sent a big bubble toward Little Gray. *Bloop!* Why, this might be more fun than the lagoon!

Little Gray blasted bubbles out of his blowhole.
Burbleburble. Then, he hit the water with his flukes.
Slap, slap, slap! Finally, Little Gray jumped as high
as he could. *SMACK!*

For Creative Minds

Whale Surfacing

Whale surfacing behavior describes the different ways that whales come to the surface. The most important reason to come to the surface is to give the whale a chance to breathe. The way whales surface can help them see what is around them, communicate with other whales, or scare nearby fish. Can you match the descriptions of different surfacing behaviors to the pictures of Little Gray? Answers are below.

Breaching is when a whale jumps up so high that at least 40% of its body is out of the water.

Spyhopping is when the whale holds its head up so its eyes are near or above the surface of the water. Some whales spyhop for several minutes at a time.

Lobtailing is when the whale lifts its tail up out of the water and smacks it down on the surface.

1.

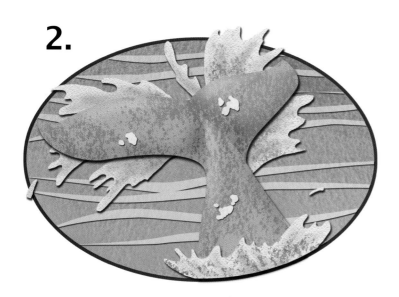

2.

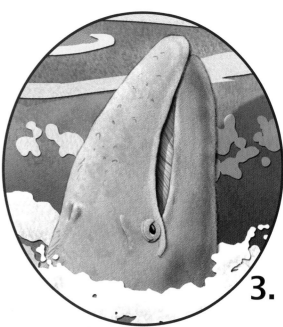

3.

Answers: 1. Breaching, 2. Lobtailing, 3. Spyhopping

Gray Whale Fun Facts

When calves are born, they are around 15 feet (4.5 meters) long. A newborn whale drinks between 50 to 80 gallons (190 to 300 liters) of milk each day.

There are currently 20,000 to 22,000 eastern gray whales. These gray whales live along the coast of North America in the Pacific Ocean. A small group of fewer than 130 gray whales live in the western Pacific and migrate along the coast of Korea. Eastern gray whales have recovered from near extinction and are not at risk of becoming endangered. Western gray whales are critically endangered.

Whales are mammals and breathe air. Gray whales have two blowholes on top of their head. These blowholes are like nostrils and are how the whales inhale and exhale.

When they are migrating south, gray whales don't sleep; they swim day and night! When gray whales sleep, they stay at the surface with their blowholes above the water.

Adult gray whales can hold their breath for up to 30 minutes. When they are resting at the surface, gray whales breathe two to three times each minute.

Gray whales can be very friendly and curious! In their winter lagoons, some gray whales approach and rub up against boats, and even allow people to touch them.

The gray-white patches on gray whales' skin are scars caused by lice and barnacles that attach to the whales. When whales are in the warmer waters of Baja, the barnacles slough off, leaving scars.

An adult gray whale's flukes (tail) measure 10 to 12 feet (3 to 3.6 meters) across.

Migration Map

Gray whales swim 10,000-13,000 miles (16,000-21,000 kilometers) each year on their round-trip migration. Calves are born in the winter in warm southern waters. Most calves are born in the waters of Baja California, a peninsula in Mexico. Some gray whale calves are born in the Southern California Bight. In the spring, the gray whales leave their winter calving grounds. They swim north along the coast, all the way to the Bering Sea and the Chukchi Sea, between Alaska and Russia. In these cool, northern waters, the whales find plenty of krill, amphipods and other small organisms to eat all summer long! Come autumn, the gray whales swim south down the coast to southern California and Mexico.

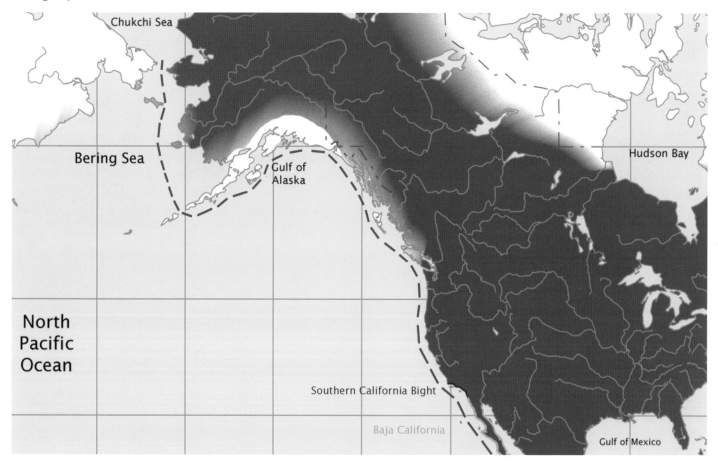

A year in the life of a gray whale:

Match the stage of the gray whales' migration to the season. Answers are below:

1. Whales feed on krill and amphipods in their arctic feeding grounds.
2. Calves are born off the coast of southern California and Baja California, in Mexico.
3. Gray whales migrate south to their calving grounds in southern California and Mexico.
4. Gray whales migrate north to their feeding grounds in the Bering and Chukchi seas.

A. Winter   B. Spring   C. Summer   D. Autumn

Whale Food

Gray whales are a kind of **baleen whale**. Baleen whales don't have teeth. Instead, they have baleen made of keratin, the same thing human hair and fingernails are made from. Baleen is a filter that traps the whale's prey. Gray whales eat small crustaceans and mollusks that live on and above the sea floor. One of gray whales' favorite foods is small, shrimplike creatures called amphipods. They also like mysid shrimp, polychaete worms and krill.

Gray whales eat by turning to one side and sucking up a mouthful of water, mud, and prey off the sea floor. They press their tongues up against the roof of their mouth to push water and mud out through the baleen while keeping the food trapped inside. Adult gray whales can eat 2,600 pounds (1,200 kilograms) of food in a day!

During the feeding months in the spring, summer, and fall, gray whales build up a thick layer of fat, called **blubber**, all over their bodies. This layer of blubber can grow up to 10 inches (25 centimeters) thick and whales can live off the fat stored in their blubber if there is no food to eat. Gray whales eat very little during their migration south in late fall and while in the winter calving grounds, so they need a thick layer of blubber to last until they return north to the primary feeding grounds in spring.

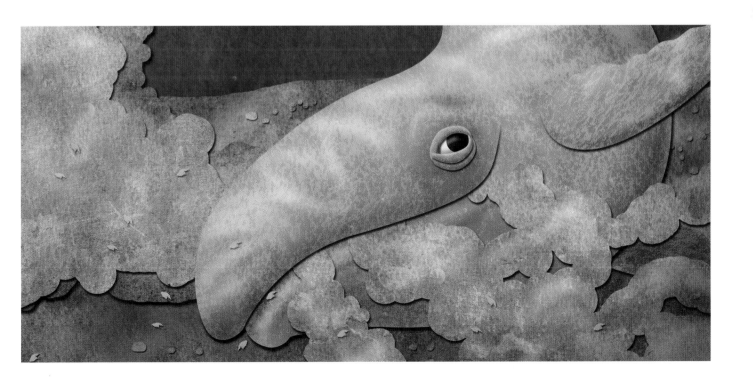

To Drew and Helena—ML
To Janna Jacobson, who loves whales—AG
Thanks to Dr. Sarah Allen, marine scientist with the National Park Service's Ocean and Coastal Resources Program, for reviewing the accuracy of the information in this book.
The author donates a percentage of her royalties to several ocean conservation organizations, including the Monterey Bay Aquarium, the American Cetacean Society, the Ocean Futures Society, the Aquarium by the Bay, and The Marine Mammal Center.

Library of Congress Cataloging-in-Publication Data

Lindsey, Marta, 1978- author.
  Little Gray's great migration / by Marta Lindsey ; illustrated by Andrea Gabriel.
      pages cm
 Audience: Ages 4-8.
  ISBN 978-1-62855-452-6 (English hardcover) -- ISBN 978-1-62855-460-1 (English pbk.) -- ISBN 978-1-62855-476-2 (English downloadable ebook) -- ISBN 978-1-62855-492-2 (English interactive dual-language ebook) -- ISBN 978-1-62855-468-7 (Spanish pbk.) -- ISBN 978-1-62855-484-7 (Spanish downloadable ebook) -- ISBN 978-1-62855-500-4 (Spanish interactive dual-language ebook) 1. Gray whale--Juvenile literature. 2. Animal migration--Juvenile literature. I. Gabriel, Andrea, illustrator. II. Title.
  QL737.C425L56 2014
  599.5'22--dc23
                                     2014011135

Translated into Spanish: Grandes migraciones de la ballena gris.
Lexile® Level: 540
key phrases for educators: adaptations, anthropomorphic, basic needs, migration, water features (ocean)

                            Bibliography:
Busch, Robert. Gray Whales, Wandering Giants. Custer, WA. Orca Book Publishers: 1998.
Darling, Jim. Gray Whales. Voyageur Press, 1999.
Gohier, Francois. A Pod of Gray Whales. Blake Publishing, 1987.
Oceanic Society. Field Guide to the Gray Whale. Seattle, WA: Sasquatch Books, 2002.
Peterson, Brenda and Linda Hogan. Sightings: The Gray Whales' Mysterious Journey. National Geographic: 2003.
Russel, Dick. Eye of the Whale: Epic Passage from Baja to Siberia. Washington, DC. Island Press: 2004.

Manufactured in China, November 2014
This product conforms to CPSIA 2008
First Printing

Arbordale Publishing
Mt. Pleasant, SC 29464
www.ArbordalePublishing.com